Mr Gumpy's Outing

John Burningham

JONATHAN CAPE, LONDON

Other books by John Burningham

BORKA (Winner of the Kate Greenaway Award in 1964)

TRUBLOFF

ABC

HUMBERT

CANNONBALL SIMP

HARQUIN

SEASONS

MR GUMPY'S MOTOR CAR

AROUND THE WORLD IN EIGHTY DAYS

WOULD YOU RATHER...

THE SHOPPING BASKET

AVOCADO BABY

GRANPA

WHERE'S JULIUS?

JOHN PATRICK NORMAN Mc HENNESSY,
    THE BOY WHO WAS ALWAYS LATE

OI! GET OFF OUR TRAIN

ALDO

Little Books

THE BABY

THE BLANKET

THE CUPBOARD

THE DOG

THE FRIEND

THE SCHOOL

THE SNOW

First published 1970
Reprinted 1974, 1978, 1985, 1990, 1991, 1993, 1996
Copyright © 1970 by John Burningham
Jonathan Cape Ltd, 20 Vauxhall Bridge Road, London SW1V 2SA
ISBN 0 224 61909 8
Printed in China
Typography and title-page design by Jan Pienkowski

This is Mr Gumpy.

Mr Gumpy owned a boat and his house
was by a river.

One day Mr Gumpy went out in his boat.

"May we come with you?" said the children.

"Yes," said Mr Gumpy,
"if you don't squabble."

"Can I come along, Mr Gumpy?"
said the rabbit.

"Yes, but don't hop about."

"I'd like a ride," said the cat.

"Very well," said Mr Gumpy.
"But you're not to chase the rabbit."

"Will you take me with you?" said the dog.

"Yes," said Mr Gumpy.
"But don't tease the cat."

"May I come, please, Mr Gumpy?"
said the pig.

"Very well, but don't muck about."

"Have you a place for me?" said the sheep.

"Yes, but don't keep bleating."

"Can we come too?" said the chickens.

"Yes, but don't flap," said Mr Gumpy.

"Can you make room for me?" said the calf.

"Yes, if you don't trample about."

"May I join you, Mr Gumpy?" said the goat.

"Very well, but don't kick."

For a little while they all went along happily but then...

The goat kicked

The calf trampled

The chickens flapped

The sheep bleated

The pig mucked about

The dog teased the cat

The cat chased the rabbit

The rabbit hopped

The children squabbled

The boat tipped...

and into the water they fell.

Then Mr Gumpy and the goat and the calf and the chickens and the sheep and the pig and the dog and the cat and the rabbit and the children all swam to the bank and climbed out to dry in the hot sun.

"We'll walk home across the fields," said Mr Gumpy. "It's time for tea."

"Goodbye," said Mr Gumpy.
"Come for a ride another day."